The Adventures of PINOCCHIO

From the original Italian story by
Carlo Collodi

Retold by
Helen Rossendale & Graham Philpot

Illustrated by
Graham Philpot

DIAL BOOKS FOR YOUNG READERS  NEW YORK

To Henrietta.
G.P.

First published in the United States 2003
by Dial Books for Young Readers
A division of Penguin Putnam Inc.
345 Hudson Street • New York, New York 10014
Published in the United Kingdom 2002
by David Bennett Books Limited • 64 Brewery Road, London N7 9NT
A member of Chrysalis Books plc
Text copyright © 2002 Helen Rossendale and Graham Philpot
Illustrations copyright © 2002 Graham Philpot
All rights reserved
Manufactured in China
1 3 5 7 9 10 8 6 4 2

Library of Congress Cataloging-in-Publication Data
Rossendale, Helen.
The adventures of Pinocchio / from the original Italian story by Carlo
Collodi ; retold by Helen Rossendale & Graham Philpot ; illustrated by Graham Philpot.
p.   cm.
Summary: Retells the adventures of a mischievous wooden puppet,
who wants more than anything else to become a real boy.
ISBN 0-8037-2919-7
[1. Fairy tales. 2. Puppets—Fiction.] I. Collodi, Carlo, 1826–1890.
II. Philpot, Graham. III. Title.   PZ8.R6685 Ad 2003
[E]—dc21   2002151067

The art for this book was created with linework in
waterproof ink and a watercolor paint wash.

CHAPTER ONE—PAGE 4

Geppetto's Puppet

CHAPTER TWO—PAGE 20

Five Gold Coins

CHAPTER THREE—PAGE 36

The Blue Fairy

CHAPTER FOUR—PAGE 52

Lost and Found

CHAPTER FIVE—PAGE 62

From School to Playland

CHAPTER SIX—PAGE 80

From Donkeydom to Boyhood

CHAPTER ONE

Geppetto's Puppet

Once upon a time there was a piece of wood.
It belonged to an old carpenter whom everyone called
Mr. Cherry because he had a small, shiny red nose.

One wintry afternoon, Mr. Cherry picked up that
piece of wood to carve it into a table leg. He lifted his
axe to slice the rough bark from the wood, but as he did
so, he heard a tiny voice.

"Please don't strike me," it begged. Mr. Cherry
looked all around, but he was quite alone.

"Must be my imagination," he muttered, and struck
the wood with his axe.

This time the voice cried out. "Stop! You're hurting
me." The voice had come from the piece of wood!
Mr. Cherry was so shocked, he collapsed onto the floor
and his cherry-red nose turned blue.

Just then there was a knock at the door.

"Stop! You're hurting me," cried the piece of wood.

It was Mr. Cherry's old friend Geppetto. He too was a carpenter, and everyone called him Mr. Omelette-Head because he wore a yellow wig. How Geppetto hated this name!

"Whatever is the matter?" exclaimed Geppetto, finding his friend lying in a heap. Mr. Cherry began mumbling a reply, but Geppetto was far too excited to listen. "I've had a fine idea," he announced. "I'm going to make a puppet that will dance and turn somersaults in the air."

"Bravo, Mr. Omelette-Head!" cried the piece of wood. Of course, Geppetto thought Mr. Cherry had said these words, and the two old men began to argue. Then they started to fight...but their scuffle did not last long, and soon they were shaking hands.

As a friendly gesture, Mr. Cherry gave Geppetto his mysterious piece of wood.

"Bravo, Mr. Omelette-Head!" cried the piece of wood.

"Oh, my!" gasped Geppetto. "You're such a naughty puppet."

Back in his humble workshop, Geppetto began to carve his puppet from that mysterious piece of wood. "I shall call him Pinocchio and he shall be my son," said Geppetto. But as he worked, strange things started to happen.

As he carved the eyes, they began to blink. As he carved the nose, it began to grow. As he carved the mouth, it laughed at him and stuck out its tongue.

Geppetto could not believe his eyes, but carried on working nonetheless. He carved the body, the neck, the arms, the hands, legs, and the feet. As Geppetto put the puppet together, it reached out and grabbed his wig.

"Oh, my!" gasped Geppetto. "You're such a naughty puppet."

As he spoke, Pinocchio jumped down onto the floor, danced around the room, and ran out into the street.

Geppetto chased after Pinocchio, but he was too slow.

"Catch him, someone. Catch him!" cried Geppetto. The onlookers just laughed in amazement.

Pinocchio clattered over the cobbles like a galloping horse . . . and ran straight into the arms of a policeman. Picking Pinocchio up by his nose, the policeman returned him to Geppetto.

"Just wait until I get you home!" scolded Geppetto, shaking his naughty puppet.

A small crowd had now gathered, but their laughter had turned to jeers. They accused Geppetto of cruelty to puppets. So the policeman ordered Geppetto to let Pinocchio go, and he led the old man away to spend the night in prison, leaving Pinocchio to skip home.

He returned the puppet to Geppetto.

Back home, Pinocchio flung himself into Geppetto's old armchair. Suddenly, he heard a clicking sound. He looked up and saw a cricket creeping along the wall.

"Who are you?" asked Pinocchio.

"Why, I am the talking cricket," replied the little green insect. "And I have a warning for you. If you are rude and ungrateful to your father, and if you run away from home, then you shall come to no good."

"Oh, be quiet, you miserable, croaking cricket," snapped Pinocchio. Then, grabbing a mallet, he hurled it at the wall. Now, Pinocchio had meant nothing more than to startle the cricket, but the mallet struck him squarely and the poor creature, who had been simply trying to offer some good advice, was flattened.

"Why, I am the talking cricket."

Pinocchio was beginning to feel hungry. Geppetto's larder was bare, so he walked into the village to ask for food. It was a dark, stormy night, and each time he knocked on someone's door, he was greeted with angry cries to go away. Pinocchio trudged back home. Exhausted, soaking wet, and still *very* hungry, he sat by the fire to dry himself. Before long he was fast asleep.

The next thing he knew, it was morning and Pinocchio was woken by Geppetto's angry voice.

"I'm home!" he cried. "But no thanks to you." Then Geppetto looked down at Pinocchio's feet and saw two burned stumps. He began to sob, "Whatever has happened to you, my little boy?"

Pinocchio told Geppetto his sorry story: how he had not meant to kill the cricket, how no one had given him food, and how his feet had burned to cinders as he slept.

He sat by the fire to dry himself and fell asleep.

"I promise I won't run away ever again, Daddy," said Pinocchio.

Geppetto took three pears from his pocket and gave them to his dear little puppet. Pinocchio was so hungry that he gobbled them up and left nothing for Geppetto. Then the old man carved two new feet and glued them to Pinocchio's legs.

"Oh, thank you, Daddy!" cried Pinocchio. "I promise I won't run away ever again. I'll be a good puppet and I'll go to school. But I'll need some clothes to wear."

So Geppetto made Pinocchio a fine suit out of colored paper, a pair of shoes out of bark, and a hat out of stale bread.

"There's just one other thing I need," said Pinocchio. "If I am to go to school, I will need an exercise book."

Now, Geppetto had no money, but he loved his little puppet so much that he went straight out, sold his only coat, and bought Pinocchio an exercise book.

CHAPTER TWO

Five Gold Coins

It was snowing when Pinocchio set off for school.

Today I shall learn to read, he thought. Tomorrow I shall learn to write, and the day after that I shall learn my numbers. Then I shall be able to earn lots of money and buy my daddy a new coat!

But as he approached the village square, he was distracted by music and a man announcing:

"The Greatest Puppet Show on Earth!"

In an instant, Pinocchio forgot his promise to Geppetto and he sold his schoolbook for just two cents, the price of a ticket for the show. Full of excitement, he stepped into the tent. He gave not a single thought to his poor father, shivering at home . . . without a coat.

Pinocchio was quite mesmerized by the sounds coming from the tent.

The show had already started and the audience cheered as Harlequin and Punchinello clowned around on stage. But as soon as the puppets caught sight of Pinocchio, they called out, "Why, if it isn't Pinocchio! Come and join your wooden brothers and sisters!"

Pinocchio leaped onto the stage and the puppets crowded around him. The audience became restless. "Get on with the show!" they demanded.

At that moment, the showman appeared. He was a huge ugly man with a long black beard. "Who has dared to disturb my show?" he boomed, pointing an angry finger at Pinocchio. "Tonight," he continued, "you will come to my tent to explain yourselves. But now, ladies and gentlemen . . . on with the show!"

"Who has dared to disturb my show?" boomed the showman.

In the evening, the puppets led Pinocchio to the tent where the showman was preparing his supper.

"Harlequin! Punchinello!" he bellowed. "Throw that miserable Pinocchio on the fire!"

"But, but, master," pleaded Punchinello. "Why?"

"Because I said so!" snapped the angry showman.

The two puppets reluctantly pulled Pinocchio toward the flames: They were too scared to disobey. Pinocchio wriggled furiously and cried out, "Oh, save me, Daddy! Save me!"

On hearing these words, the showman suddenly softened. Remembering his own father with great fondness, he took pity on Pinocchio and spared him from the flames.

"Tell me," he said. "Does your daddy love you?"

"Oh, yes!" replied Pinocchio. "We have no money, but yesterday, in the middle of winter, he sold his only coat to buy me a schoolbook. That's how much he loves me."

"Here, take these five gold coins home to him," said the showman. "You are lucky to have such a father."

"Throw Pinocchio on the fire!" he bellowed.

In the morning, Pinocchio woke up thinking he must have had a dream. But the five gold coins that he was clutching were very real. He thanked the showman a thousand times, said a fond farewell to all the puppets, and set out for home.

He had not gone far, when he met a lame fox and a blind cat, begging by the roadside.

"Good morning, little puppet," whined the fox. "Can you spare us a penny or two?"

Foolishly, Pinocchio told the strangers that he had five gold coins for his father and that he was returning home to go to school.

"School!" hissed the cat. "You don't want to go to school. It is studying that made us lame and blind!"

"Why don't you come with us?" asked the fox. "We know a place where you could turn those five gold coins into five *thousand* gold coins!"

"Can you spare us a penny or two?" whined the fox.

". . . and overnight they grow into money trees," said the fox.

"This place," continued the fox, "is called the Field of Miracles. It's a magical place where you bury your coins, and overnight they grow into money trees!"

Pinocchio's eyes became as wide as saucers. *With that sort of money I could buy Daddy one hundred new coats and a schoolbook for every day of the year!* he thought. He turned to the fox and the cat and said, "Yes! I shall come with you."

After walking all day, the three decided to stop off at the Red Crab Inn. The fox and the cat feasted on fish, chicken, rabbit, partridge eggs, frogs' legs, lizards' tails, and cheese, but Pinocchio, whose mind was on other things, only nibbled at some bread.

"Now let us go to our rooms and rest," said the fox. "We'll continue our journey at midnight."

As the clock struck twelve, Pinocchio leaped out of bed. "But where are the fox and the cat?" he asked. The innkeeper told Pinocchio his companions had already gone and then asked for one gold coin as payment for the bill.

Quite bemused, Pinocchio stumbled out into the darkness. He was drawn to a strange green glow in the trees.

"I am the ghost of the talking cricket," it said. "Do not trust the fox and the cat." But Pinocchio refused to listen and the ghost faded away, murmuring, "Beware of robbers, Pinocchio. Beware!"

"Robbers indeed!" scoffed Pinocchio, but just as he said these words, two black figures wrapped in coal sacks came bounding out of the darkness toward him. Quick as a flash, Pinocchio hid the four coins in his shoe and, as he stood up, the attackers grabbed him from behind.

"Your money or your life!" they cried.

"But I have no money!" protested Pinocchio.

"Your money or your life!" cried the robbers.

The robbers did not believe him, and this time they shouted, "Your money or your *father's* life!"

Their threat made Pinocchio very angry indeed. He stamped on the big one's bushy tail and bit the little one's furry paw, and ran for his life into the woods. He had no time to realize who these robbers really were!

At the edge of the woods he came upon a little white cottage. At the window stood a beautiful young girl with blue hair. But she did not see Pinocchio, and she closed the shutters. Moments later, the robbers pounced on Pinocchio again, but this time he was too exhausted to resist. They bound him up with ropes and tied him to a big oak tree.

"We shall come back tomorrow," they sneered. "By then you will tell us where your gold coins are."

They tied him to a big oak tree.

CHAPTER THREE

The Blue Fairy

In the morning, the child with the blue hair looked out of the window and saw poor Pinocchio hanging from the tree. At once, she clapped her hands and a great falcon appeared.

"What is your command, Blue Fairy?" he asked.

"Fly over to the oak tree and loosen that poor puppet from his ropes," she said. Then, clapping her hands again, the blue fairy summoned a magnificent poodle. He was dressed as a coachman in a raspberry-red tailcoat and chocolate-brown breeches.

She commanded him to fetch Pinocchio in his grandest coach. It was made of golden pastry lined with strawberry cushions stuffed with custard and cream and pulled by a hundred sugar-white mice.

The blue fairy commanded the poodle to fetch poor Pinocchio.

As soon as the poodle returned with Pinocchio, the blue fairy laid him gently on a bed. Then she called for the best doctors in the neighborhood—a crow, an owl, and a talking cricket. These wise doctors could not agree whether Pinocchio was dead or alive, but the cricket turned to the blue fairy and spoke gravely.

"Here is a most disobedient, wayward son who will surely make his father die of a broken heart," he said.

Suddenly, Pinocchio broke into sorrowful sobs. "He's alive!" sighed the blue fairy. She sent the doctors away and then, speaking softly, asked Pinocchio how he came to be hanging from a tree.

Pinocchio told the blue fairy everything. How the showman had given him five gold coins, how he had been tricked by the fox and the cat, and how he had been chased and tied up by two masked attackers.

The cricket spoke gravely to the blue fairy.

"Where are your gold coins now?" asked the blue fairy kindly.

"I've lost them," answered Pinocchio. But this was a lie, for he had them in his shoe, and as soon as he spoke these words, his nose grew two inches longer!

"Where did you lose them?" asked the fairy.

"In the woods," said Pinocchio. A second lie. His nose grew again!

"Then we shall search for them and they shall be found," said the blue fairy.

"Oh, no," he replied. "I remember now, the robbers stole them." At this third lie, his nose grew so long that it touched the windowpane!

The fairy looked at him and laughed.

"Why are you laughing at me?" asked Pinocchio.

"I am laughing at the lies you have told, Pinocchio. For each time you lie, your nose grows a little longer!"

"Each time you lie," said the blue fairy, "your nose gets longer!"

A thousand woodpeckers flew into the room.

Pinocchio began to whimper with shame. He even tried to run from the room, but his nose was too long for him to get through the door! The fairy left him alone for a while to teach him a lesson, but then she clapped her hands and a thousand woodpeckers flew into the room. They pecked away at Pinocchio's nose until it was back to its normal size.

"How good you are to me," said Pinocchio. "I love you."

"I love you too," answered the fairy. "I shall be your darling sister." Then the fairy promised to bring Pinocchio's father to the cottage that very evening. Full of joy, Pinocchio ran outside to wait for Geppetto.

But whom should he meet instead? The wicked fox and cat! For a second time, Pinocchio was fooled by their deceitful words and agreed to go with them to the Field of Miracles.

When they reached the lonely spot, Pinocchio knelt down to dig four small holes for his four gold coins. Then he covered them with earth.

"Now you must go away for twenty minutes," explained the fox. "When you come back, you'll see the first green shoots already covered in gold coins."

"Thank you so much," cried Pinocchio, waving good-bye to the fox and the cat.

But when Pinocchio returned, there were no green shoots. There was only a scraggy parrot who squawked rudely and told Pinocchio that the fox and the cat had dug up the coins and then run away. Pinocchio simply could not believe it. He dug a hole as big as a haystack, but alas, the parrot was right. The coins were gone!

He dug a hole as big as a haystack.

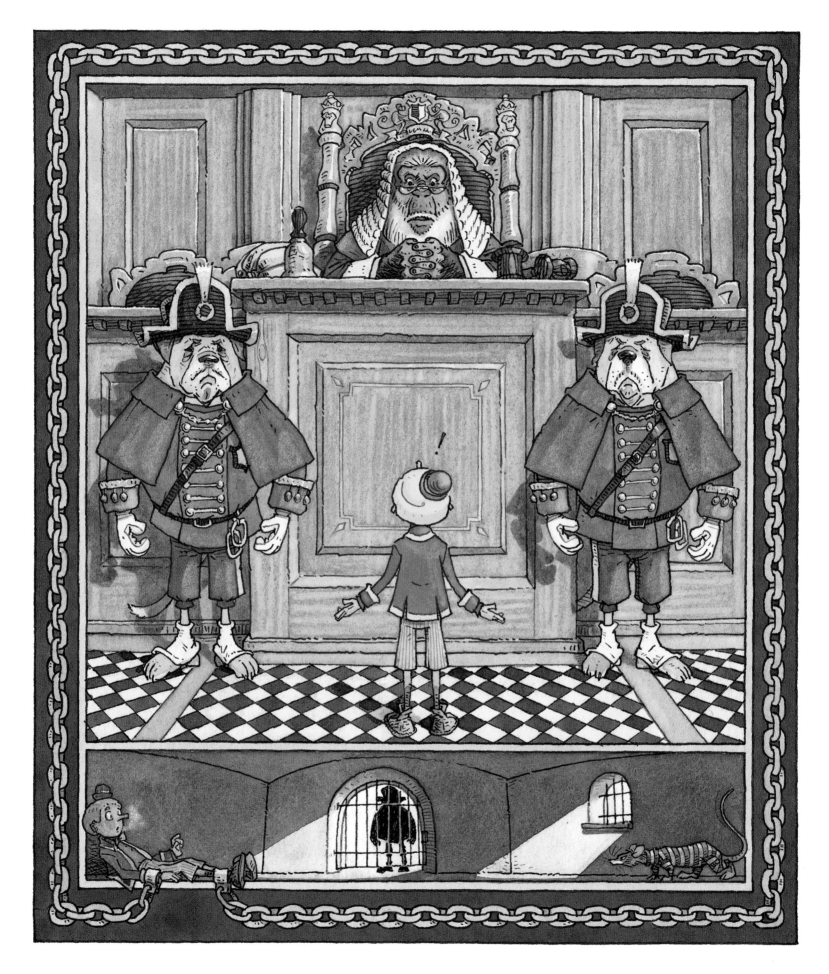

"This fellow has been robbed," declared the judge. "Take him to prison."

In desperation, Pinocchio ran to a nearby town to tell the judge about the evil robbers. The judge, a portly gorilla, listened patiently to Pinocchio's story. Then, clearing his throat, he announced, "This poor fellow has been robbed. Take him to prison immediately."

After four long months in jail in this strange, cruel town, Pinocchio was set free. Without losing a second, he left the town and took the lane that led to the fairy's cottage. It was a warm, sunny afternoon, and Pinocchio's throat felt quite parched as he hurried along. Suddenly, he caught sight of a field of vines and, as nimble as ever, Pinocchio leaped over the hedge to pick some juicy grapes. But as he landed, there was a loud CRACK! His legs had been caught in a rusty iron trap.

Pinocchio screamed for help. And the farmer, who had set the trap, came running over to see his catch.

"So, little puppet!" he grunted. "It's you who has been stealing my chickens!"

"No, sir!" pleaded Pinocchio. "I only wanted a few grapes."

The farmer opened the trap, seized Pinocchio, and dragged him to the farmyard. He chained Pinocchio to a kennel and bellowed, "You shall be my new guard dog."

Poor Pinocchio! He was cold and frightened. He lay down and cried himself to sleep.

Later that night, he was woken by voices. In the darkness Pinocchio saw four prowling polecats. One of them approached Pinocchio and gruffly warned him, "Be quiet, or else!"

But when the polecats had skulked into the chicken coop, Pinocchio quickly bolted the door and barked as loud as he could. The farmer rushed out in his nightshirt. He was so pleased that Pinocchio had caught the chicken thieves that he hugged him warmly and let him go.

Pinocchio ran through the night to the fairy's house.

Later that night, Pinocchio was woken by voices.

CHAPTER FOUR

Lost and Found

When he reached the edge of the woods, there was no sign of the little white cottage. Instead, where it had stood, there was a simple white grave. Pinocchio fell to his knees and burst into floods of tears.

The inscription engraved on the marble read:

HERE LIES
THE BLUE-HAIRED CHILD
WHO DIED OF SORROW
ON BEING DESERTED
BY HER LITTLE BROTHER,
PINOCCHIO

Although Pinocchio could not read the words, he knew at once the horrible meaning of the little grave. He had lost his beloved blue fairy.

"Please, dear fairy," he sobbed, "come back to me and tell me where I may find my daddy."

Just then, a pigeon flew over Pinocchio's head. It was as large as a turkey. "I have come to take you to your father," cooed the pigeon. "Climb onto my back!"

"I have come to take you to your father," cooed the pigeon.

Holding tightly to the pigeon's feathers, Pinocchio was whisked into the air.

"Your father is at sea," said the pigeon. "He has made a little boat so that he might cross the ocean and search the whole world for you." The pigeon flew all day until, at dusk, they reached the coast. It was a stormy night and Pinocchio saw a tiny boat being tossed by the mountainous waves. Without a moment's hesitation, he dived into the water and swam as fast as he could toward the boat.

Pinocchio swam all night, but he could not reach his father. By daybreak, he could swim no more and he was washed up on the shores of an island.

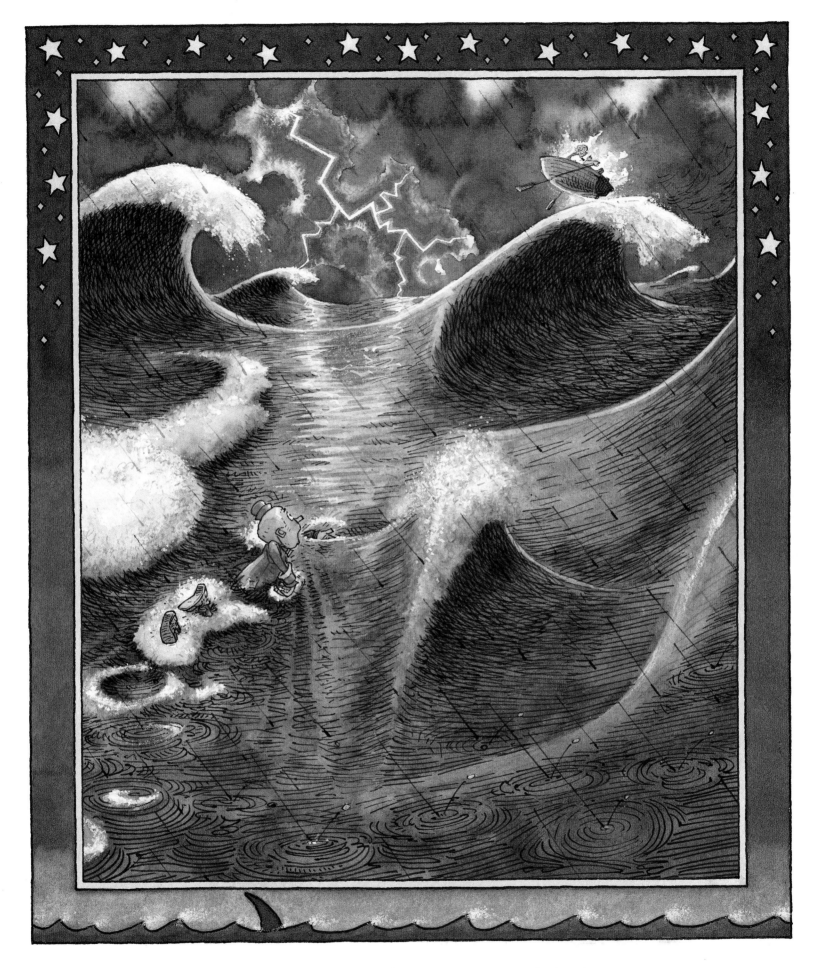

He swam as fast as he could toward the boat.

"Have you seen my daddy?" pleaded Pinocchio.

While he was waiting for his clothes to dry, Pinocchio sat on a rock and stared out to sea. Suddenly, a friendly dolphin popped its head above the waves.

"Have you seen my daddy?" pleaded Pinocchio.

"No," said the dolphin. "But there is a great shark that lurks in these waters, as big as a five-story house and with a mouth as deep and wide as a railway tunnel. I fear it has swallowed up your father."

Pinocchio got dressed and walked sadly toward the town in the middle of the island. A little woman, her head covered by a scarf, was coming toward him carrying two buckets of water. Pinocchio asked her politely for a drink.

"Gladly," said the little woman. Then she invited Pinocchio to her house for something to eat. "For you must be hungry too," she said.

The woman set down a bowl of hearty soup and a basket of bread. When he had finished eating, Pinocchio looked up to thank the kind woman. He saw her smile and knew her at once.

"Blue Fairy!" he cried. "You have come back to me!"

"Yes," she replied. "Because I could see how truly sorry you were to have lost me." The fairy was just as lovely as ever, but she was no longer a little girl.

"You have grown into a beautiful woman," said Pinocchio. "From now on I shall call you Mommy." Then he whispered, "Will I ever grow up into a real boy?"

"Yes," said the fairy. "If you are good, always tell the truth, and study hard, then I promise that one day you will find your father and become a real boy."

This book belongs to Pinocchio

I must bee ghood
I must be good
I must be good
and tell the trukth.
I must be good
I must be good
I must be good
and tell the truth.
I must be good

"Blue Fairy—you have come back to me!" cried Pinocchio.

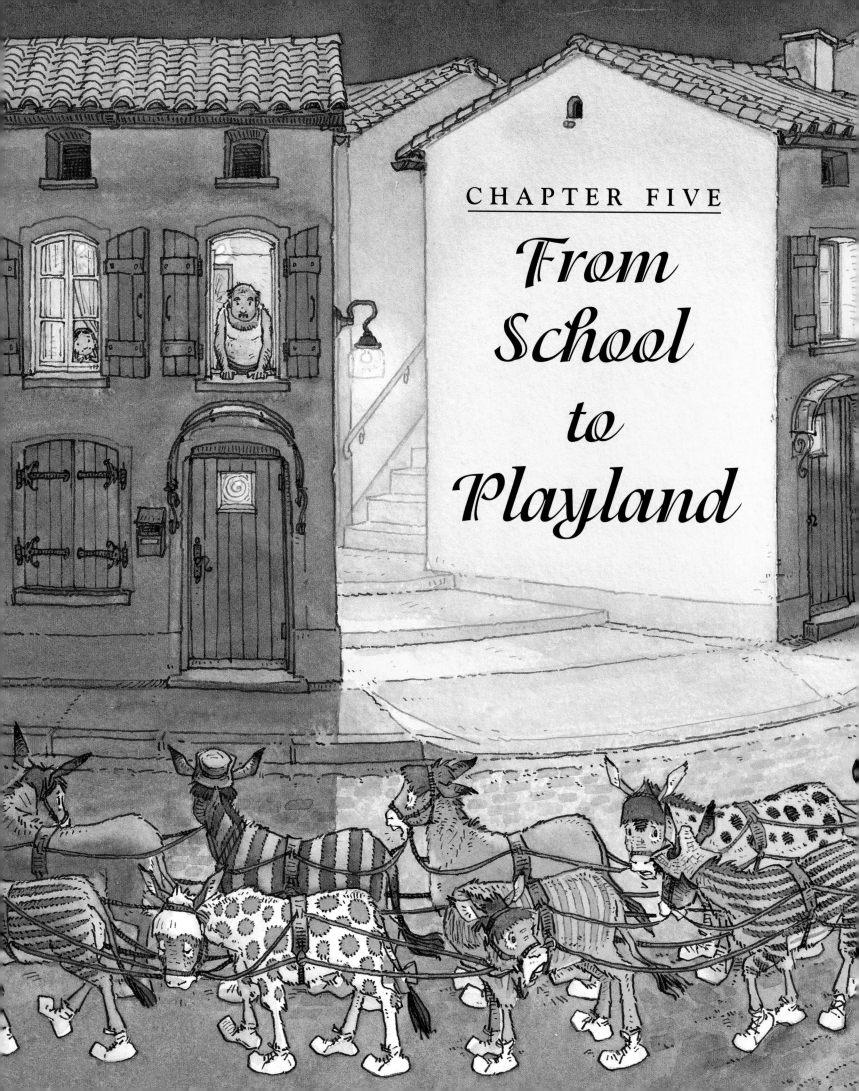

CHAPTER FIVE

From School to Playland

$\mathcal{P}$inocchio started school. He was determined not to let the blue fairy down and he worked very hard. But alas, not all of his classmates were as studious. In fact, some of them were very naughty indeed and they would often tease and bully poor Pinocchio for working so hard.

One morning, as Pinocchio walked to school, he met a gang of these naughty classmates.

"A shark as big as a mountain has been spotted in the sea," they cried. "We're going to the beach to look. Why don't you come too?"

Pinocchio wondered if this could be the shark that had swallowed up his father, and part of him wanted to go with these children to the beach. But he knew that he mustn't be late for school.

"There's a shark as big as a mountain in the sea!" cried the gang.

"School can wait," they jeered. "Anyway, it will only take an hour."

"Oh, all right then, if you're sure," replied Pinocchio, and he ran with the children to the beach. When they got to the shore, there was no sign of the shark and the sea was as calm as a duck pond.

"Where's the shark?" asked Pinocchio, turning to his classmates.

"Perhaps he's having breakfast," snickered one of them.

"Yes. Geppetto and chips!" giggled another. And they all roared with laughter. It was then that Pinocchio knew that his classmates had played a nasty trick on him and he lost his temper. An angry fight broke out. In the turmoil, a heavy leather-bound book struck one of the boys and he fell with a thud onto the sand.

Realizing what they had done, the others ran off, leaving Pinocchio with his wounded classmate.

An angry fight broke out.

"Little puppet, are you responsible for this?" demanded the policemen.

Just at that moment, two policemen came striding along the beach. There was a big police dog at their side.

"What have we here?" said one of the officers. "Little puppet, are you responsible for this boy's injuries?"

"N-n-no, sir," stammered Pinocchio.

"I think you had better come to the police station to explain yourself," grunted the other officer. And with that, they left the injured boy with some fishermen and marched Pinocchio back into town.

How ashamed I would be if the blue fairy saw me now, thought Pinocchio. He struggled free from their grasp, and ran back across the beach and into the sea.

The police dog bounded after him, but it could not swim. It splashed furiously toward Pinocchio, but, in the deeper water, it began to sink.

"Help!" barked the dog.

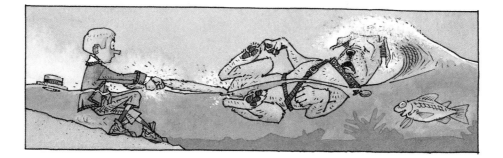

Pinocchio had his chance to escape, but he could not let the poor dog drown, so he grabbed hold of its tail and pulled it back to the shore.

"You have saved my life," panted the dog. "I shall never forget your kindness." Then it let Pinocchio go and limped off toward the town.

Pinocchio waded back into the water and swam toward the next bay. But before he could reach the rocks, he became entangled in a huge net with hundreds of flapping fish. Suddenly, the net was hauled onto the shore by a strange-looking fisherman. He dragged it into his cave, where a cauldron of oil was bubbling over an open fire.

He tossed his catch, one by one, in flour and fried them until they were crispy and golden. Pinocchio cowered in terror at the bottom of the net, awaiting his turn.

He became entangled in a huge fishing net.

"Aha," boomed the fisherman. "I've never had puppetfish before!"

Pinocchio screamed and struggled, but it was useless, and in an instant he had been smothered in flour. The fisherman was just about to drop him into the cauldron when the police dog came charging into the cave and seized Pinocchio from the fisherman's grasp.

"It was the smell of delicious fried fish that brought me here," woofed the dog. "But then I heard your screams and knew you were in danger. Climb onto my back and I'll take you home."

Back home, the blue fairy sat Pinocchio down at the kitchen table and looked at him solemnly. "I am very saddened that you did not go to school today," she said. "You must never let me down like this again."

"I won't. I won't," said Pinocchio. "I promise!"

"Aha, I've never had puppetfish before!" boomed the fisherman.

For a whole year, Pinocchio kept his promise. He went to school every day and he was always top of the class. At the end of the summer term, he came home with a big silver cup for being the best pupil of the year. The blue fairy was very, very proud of him.

"Tomorrow, Pinocchio," she said, smiling, "will be the day that you become a real boy. And to celebrate, I shall prepare a wonderful breakfast for you and all your friends."

She gave Pinocchio a bundle of invitations for his friends and he skipped down the street to deliver them. As he turned a corner, he saw his good friend Luciano sitting on the curb.

"Hello," said Pinocchio. "What are you doing?"

"I'm waiting for the coach to take me to Playland," he replied. "Do you want to come with me?"

"I'm waiting for the coach to take me to Playland," said Luciano.

Tomorrow Pinocchio will become a real boy.

You are invited to a very special Breakfast Party to celebrate this wonderful day.

"No, thank you," said Pinocchio politely. "I have all these invitations to deliver. Tomorrow I'm going to become a real boy, and to celebrate, I'm having a very special breakfast party."

"But Playland is much more fun than silly old breakfast parties!" said Luciano. "Look! Here comes the coach now!"

And sure enough, a coach came rumbling into view. It was pulled by twenty-four of the strangest-looking donkeys Pinocchio had ever seen. As you might expect, some were gray and brown, but others were multicolored with spots or stripes and, the oddest thing of all, they were all wearing white leather boots.

The coach itself was crammed with children and alongside it strode the coachman, who was broader than he was tall, with a small, round face as red as a tomato.

The coach was pulled by twenty-four of the strangest-looking donkeys.

Luciano clambered onto the crowded coach. Pinocchio hesitated, but he couldn't stop thinking about all the wonderful toys and games there would be in Playland. In a flash, he forgot his promise to the blue fairy, threw his invitations into the air, and jumped onto the nearest donkey.

As the donkeys moved off, Pinocchio thought he heard his donkey say: "Don't go, Pinocchio, don't go." But its words were drowned out by the children's laughter, and Pinocchio soon forgot its warning.

When they reached Playland, Pinocchio leaped off his donkey. By now it was crying and it spoke again, "Please don't go in, Pinocchio. You'll end up like me!" But Pinocchio ignored the donkey's warning. He'd already joined the mad rush through the gates of Playland.

Pinocchio spent five fabulous months in Playland. Every day there were continual games and pastimes. All kinds of entertainers came to amuse the children and the place was overflowing with happiness.

Pinocchio joined the mad rush through the gates of Playland.

CHAPTER SIX

From Donkeydom to Boyhood

One morning, Pinocchio had a nasty surprise. When he looked in the bathroom mirror, he discovered that he had grown . . . donkey ears! Pinocchio began to cry: He felt so ashamed. He pulled a bag over his ears and sneaked outside to go to Luciano's house.

"It's all Luciano's fault," he muttered. "I should never have come with him to Playland!"

When Luciano opened his door, Pinocchio gasped to see that he too had a bag on his head. When they realized they *both* had donkey ears, they laughed and laughed. But then the strangest thing happened. They began to walk on all fours and make loud braying noises. In no time at all, they had both become donkeys!

Just at that moment, the coachman arrived and, throwing a rough loop of rope around each of their necks, he took them to market. That was the last Pinocchio ever saw of Luciano.

In no time at all, they had both become donkeys!

Pinocchio learned to dance and jump through hoops.

As for Pinocchio, he was sold to a circus ringmaster. Circus life was hard. He was kept in a dingy stable and fed hay and straw. Every day, Pinocchio spent hours learning how to jump through hoops and dance the polka. Then came his first performance. The crowd loved his routine and the ringmaster lifted the hoop higher and higher.

But then disaster struck. The hoop was just too high and Pinocchio fell to the ground with a thud.

"I don't want any lame donkeys in my circus!" bellowed the ringmaster, so he took Pinocchio back to the market.

"Old nag going cheap!" he hollered.

"I'll give you five pennies," grunted a rough-looking fellow. "I'll use his skin to repair the big drum in the village band."

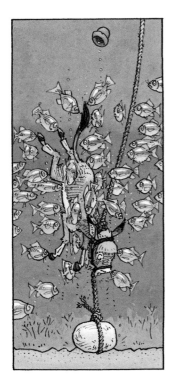

Pinocchio's new owner led him to the shore, tied a stone around his neck, and pushed him into the water. "I'll pull you back up when you're drowned," he cackled.

Imagine this ruffian's surprise when, an hour later, he pulled the rope and hauled out of the water not a dead donkey—but a talking puppet! He was flabbergasted.

"A shoal of fish nibbled away my donkey skin!" shouted Pinocchio, full of joy. And with that, he swam away.

Soon Pinocchio caught sight of a goat standing on a rock. It had a beautiful blue, curly coat—just like the blue fairy's hair—and it was pointing toward a huge shark in the distance. Pinocchio knew this must be the shark that had swallowed his daddy.

"Hurry, little puppet!" bleated the goat. "Swim for your life." Pinocchio swam as fast as he could, but the monstrous fish was too quick and swallowed poor Pinocchio in one massive gulp.

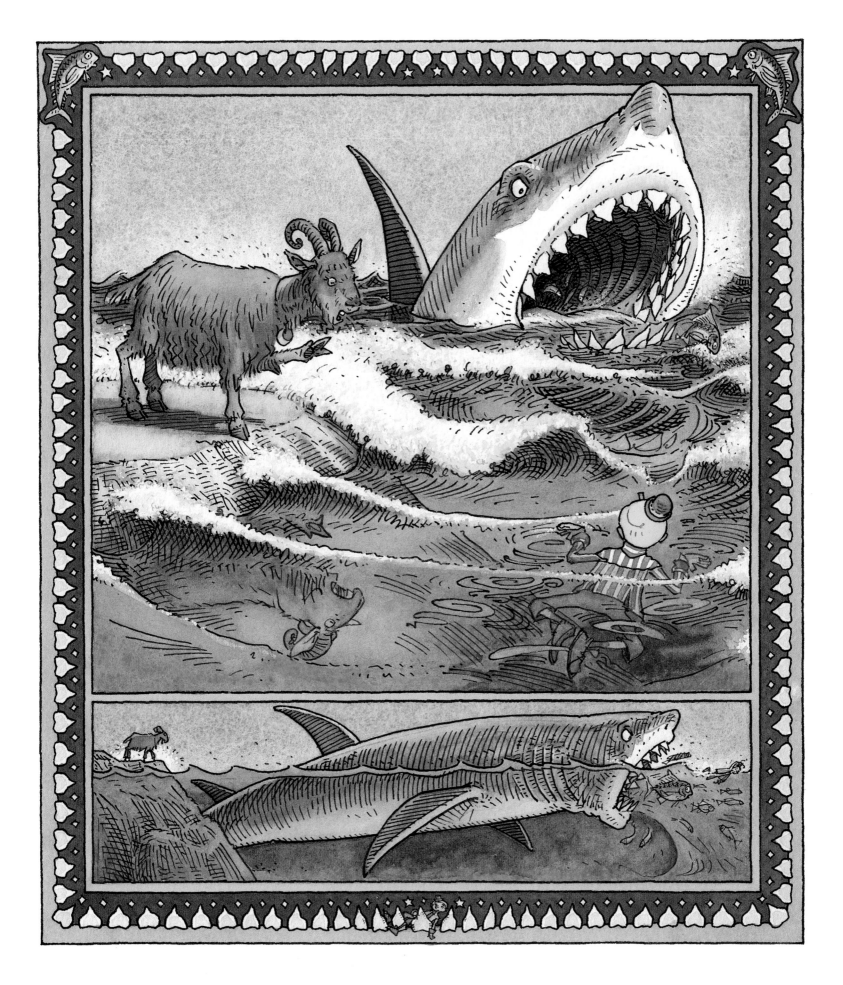

"Hurry little puppet," bleated the goat. *"Swim for your life."*

Inside the shark, Pinocchio found himself in a long, dark, cavernous tunnel, and in the gloom he caught sight of a tuna fish.

"I've been swallowed up too!" moaned the fish. "We will surely waste away and die."

"I'm not going to die!" said Pinocchio defiantly.

Then, in the darkness, he saw a flickering light. He walked steadily toward it, his footsteps echoing as he went. As he drew closer, Pinocchio saw a figure sitting by candlelight at a small table. The old man turned slowly toward Pinocchio. It was Geppetto!

"Daddy, I've found you at last!" cried the little puppet as he ran to hug his father.

Geppetto could hardly speak, he was so overcome with joy. Father and son stayed in each other's arms for a very long time and, through his tears of happiness, Pinocchio told Geppetto about every one of his sorry adventures from that fateful day when he sold his schoolbook outside the puppet theater.

Then, in the darkness, he saw a flickering light.

Then Geppetto told Pinocchio his story. "I've been trapped here for two years," he explained.

"But how have you kept alive?" asked Pinocchio.

"Just after I was swallowed up," replied Geppetto, "the shark gulped down a large ship and I've been living off its stores of food. But now there is very little left."

"We must find a way out!" said Pinocchio firmly. He took Geppetto's hand and they clambered back along the shark's long, bony throat. "We'll be able to get out the way we came in," Pinocchio reassured his father. When they reached its mouth, they found that the shark was sleeping with its jaws wide open and they could see the starry night beyond the rows of fearsome teeth that gleamed menacingly in the moonlight.

"B-b-but I can't swim," stuttered Geppetto.

"Then jump onto my back," whispered Pinocchio.

They scrambled over the teeth and then, with Geppetto clinging to his back, Pinocchio swam out into the inky-black sea.

The fearsome teeth gleamed menacingly in the moonlight.

Pinocchio quickly became very tired and he could barely swim another stroke. Then, in the nick of time, the tuna fish, who had followed them out of the shark's stomach, came along and carried them to the shore.

After resting for a little while, Pinocchio and Geppetto set off along a narrow path. They walked for hours, but then they came to a familiar cobbled street and found themselves outside . . . Geppetto's house!

Every day, from dawn till dusk, Pinocchio looked after his father, who was still very, very frail. He even made a little cart for Geppetto.

Pinocchio then took a job working for a local farmer. When he had earned enough, he bought a new coat for his father and a schoolbook for himself. He didn't have time to go to school, but he practiced reading and writing every evening after supper.

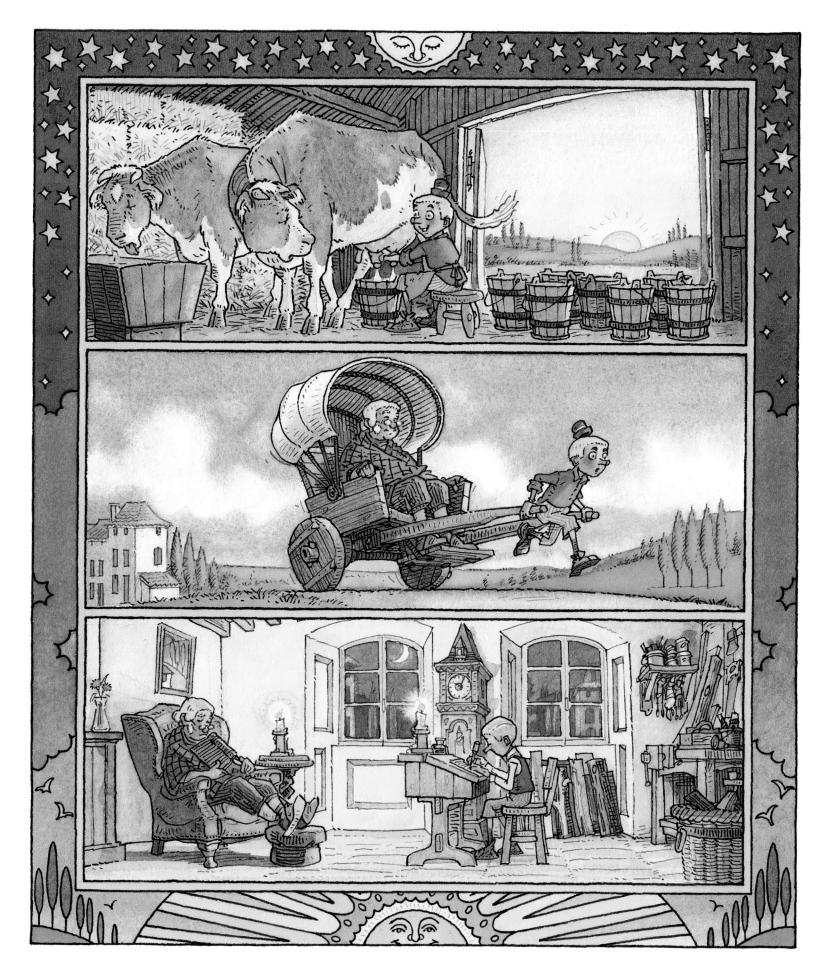

From dawn till dusk, Pinocchio looked after his father.

Little by little, Geppetto's health improved. It made Pinocchio so glad to see his father's strength return. Before long, Geppetto was well enough to start woodcarving once again.

Then, one night, Pinocchio saw the blue fairy in a dream. "You have been a brave puppet, Pinocchio," she said softly. "You rescued your father and nursed him back to health. In return for your good heart, I promise that tomorrow you will find true happiness."

The next morning, Pinocchio leaped out of bed and as usual he went to the bathroom mirror, but instead of the face of a puppet, he saw the smiling face of a little boy! Squealing with delight, he ran downstairs to find Geppetto.

Geppetto kissed his son. "It is your kindness that has turned you into a little boy," he laughed. "And I am proud to have you as my son, darling Pinocchio."

At last, Pinocchio had found true happiness . . .

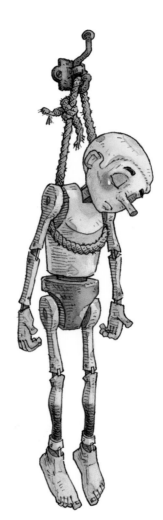

and, as for the puppet,
it was nothing more than just
a piece of wood.